First American edition published in 1987 by
Peter Bedrick Books,
125 East 23 Street,
New York,
NY 10010.

Library of Congress Cataloging-in-Publication Data available.

ISBN 0-87226-154-9

Text and illustrations copyright © 1987 Amanda Hall
First published 1987 by
Blackie and Son Ltd
7 Leicester Place
London WC2H 7BP

British Library Cataloguing in Publication Data

Hall, Amanda
    The Foolish Husbands.
    I. Title
    823'.914 [J]   PZ8.1

    ISBN 0-216-92106-6

Printed in Great Britain by Cambus Litho

THE FOOLISH
HUSBANDS

AMANDA HALL

Adapted from a Norwegian Folk Tale

BLACKIE
LONDON

BEDRICK/BLACKIE
NEW YORK

Once upon a time, in Norway, there lived two good friends called Gunhild and Margit. There was nothing they both enjoyed more than a good argument, and every time they saw each other they would argue and argue about one thing or another for hours on end.

One warm spring day, Gunhild was out walking when she met Margit. Margit had hardly time to say hello before Gunhild decided she felt like an argument.

'You know,' she said, 'there is no man in the world more stupid than my Lars. He was out in the garden yesterday, watering the potatoes, even though it was pouring with rain.'

'That's nothing!' said Margit. 'Your Lars is a genius compared to my Svein. Today when he was cutting firewood, he was sawing off the branch he was sitting on. If I hadn't come along and stopped him he would have broken his neck.'

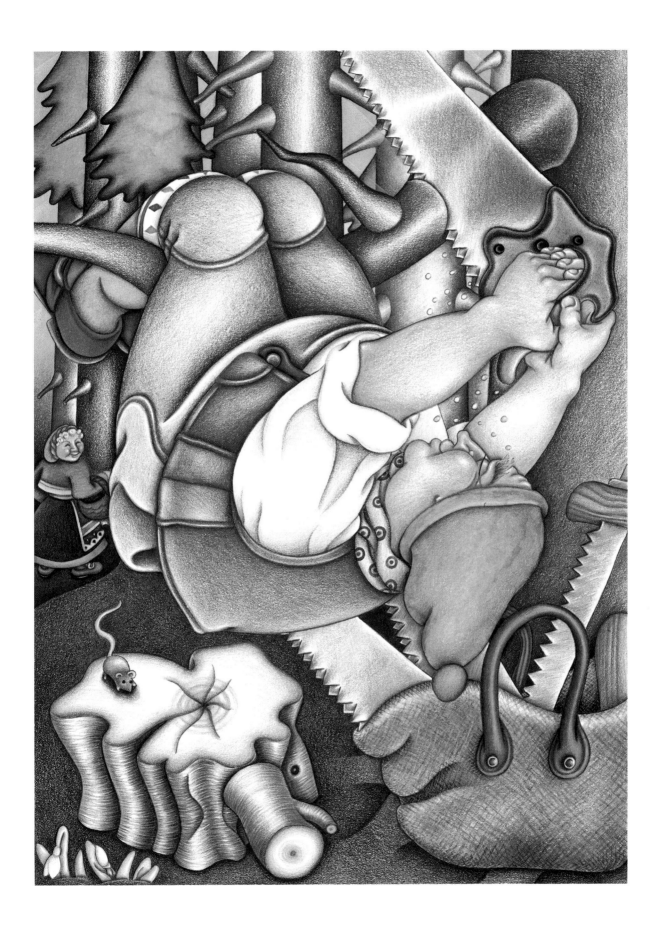

And so the big argument began. Gunhild said her husband would believe any lie, no matter how ridiculous, for he was as stupid as a troll. And Margit said that she could make her husband do anything, however stupid it was, for he had a brain

the size of a pea. On and on they argued until they decided that the best thing to do was to have a competition to see which of their husbands really was the most foolish. And, chuckling to themselves, they each went home to make their own plans.

That evening, Gunhild cooked an enormous supper. When Lars came home she piled the supper plates high with food and they sat down to eat. Now Gunhild had not eaten anything all day to make sure she was especially hungry. She finished all her first plateful of food in a flash and immediately gave Lars and herself a second helping. Lars was having trouble finishing his first helping and soon put down his fork. 'I've had enough,' he said.

'But you've eaten nothing, Lars,' said Gunhild. 'What's wrong with you — are you ill? You look very pale and tired.'

Lars looked at Gunhild wolfing down her food and thought that perhaps she was right — perhaps he was feeling a bit ill.

Meanwhile Margit had worked out her own plan. That evening, as soon as she heard the creak of the gate and Svein's tuneless whistle along the path, she sat down at her spinning-wheel. She deliberately did not put any thread on it, so that when Svein came in, there she was, spinning at an empty wheel.

'Why, Margit,' said Svein, 'you're spinning at an empty wheel. What on earth's wrong with you?'

'There's nothing wrong with me, Svein,' said Margit, 'there's something wrong with your eyes. Don't you recognize fine, expensive thread when you see it?'

Svein peered closely at the spinning-wheel. Yes, perhaps he could see some thread. It was very fine, but of course it was there. How stupid he had been not to see it!

All that night and all the following day Gunhild treated Lars like an invalid. Normally she would make him go to work however ill he felt, but this time she put a rug over his knees, propped him up with pillows and sat him by the fire. Every few minutes she would look hard at him and then go away shaking her head. Lars began to get worried. He was definitely beginning to feel very ill now.

Margit's plan was also going well. The evening after she had
fooled Svein by pretending to spin thread, she set up her loom
and pretended to weave a large piece of cloth. Then she
pretended to take the cloth off the loom and pretended to cut and

sew a complete suit for her husband. Svein sat in his chair watching her, telling himself how clever he was to have such a fine seamstress for a wife.

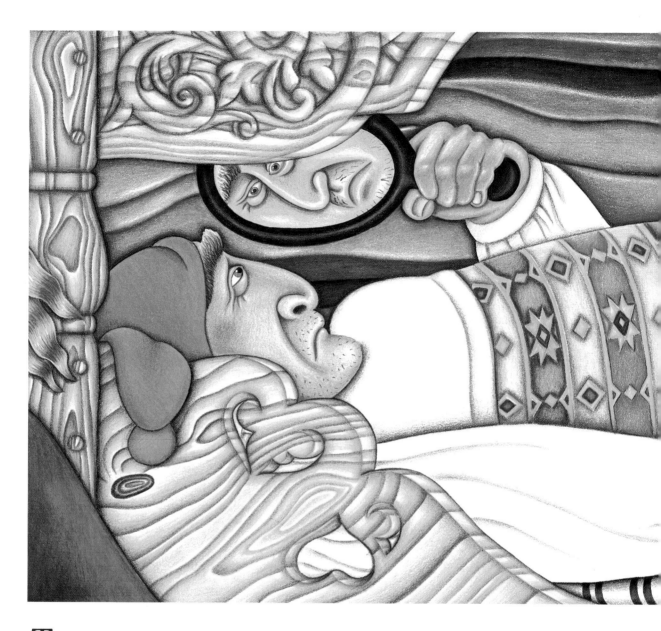

Three days later, sniffing a raw onion to make her cry, Gunhild
went to look at Lars, who by now had taken to his bed.

'God save me, Lars,' she said, 'you look as pale as a corpse.
The sickness is getting worse and worse — you won't last long at
this rate.'

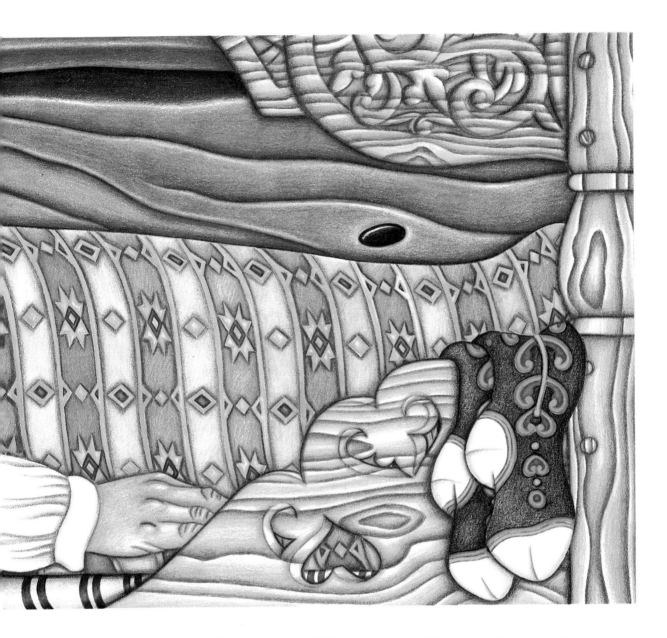

Lars weakly lifted himself from his pillow and looked at himself in the mirror. Yes, the man he saw in the reflection was certainly at death's door.

The following week, Margit announced to Svein that Lars had died and that they had to go to the burial feast. 'You'll have to look respectable for poor Lars' funeral, Svein,' she said. 'You must wear your new suit.'

While Svein was thinking how only two weeks ago he had seen his old friend Lars looking fit and well, Margit fetched his pretend suit from the loft.

'Let me help you on with it,' she said. 'The cloth is so fine that you're bound to tear it if you do it yourself.'

Svein looked at himself admiringly. 'I'm very lucky to have such a wonderful new suit,' he said. 'Thank you very much, Margit.'

By the time Margit and Svein arrived at the burial feast, the coffin was being carried to the graveside and all the guests were so drunk that they didn't even notice Svein's unusual suit. But, as the bearers lowered the coffin into the grave, Lars caught sight of Svein, standing there with no clothes on, and burst into

laughter. All the funeral guests were absolutely amazed. There was Lars, who was supposed to be dead, rolling round in his coffin with laughter; and there was Svein, standing at the graveside in nothing but his underwear! What was going on?

Finally Gunhild and Margit stepped forward, tears of laughter rolling down their cheeks, and explained the whole story to everyone.

'I don't know,' said Margit to Gunhild, still laughing, 'maybe the joke is on us — for which of us is the most stupid for marrying such a pair of idiots!' Even Lars and Svein could not help joining in all the laughter and everyone decided that, now the funeral was over, they might as well have a party instead.

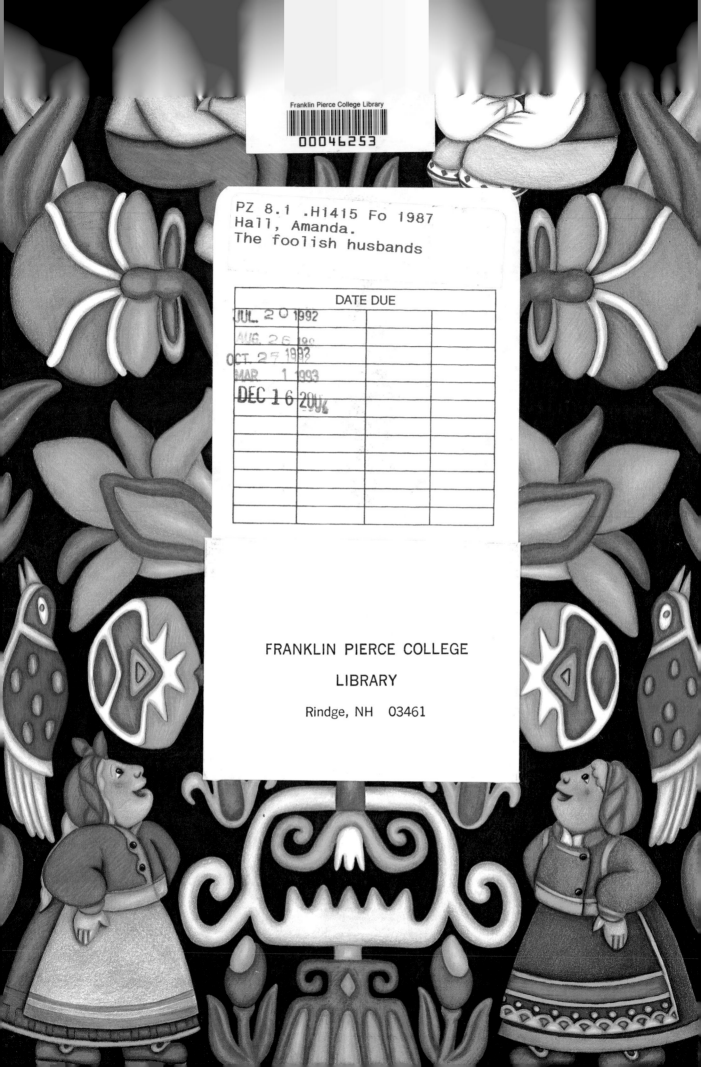